95

Night Lights

❖ A SUKKOT STORY ❖

By Barbara Diamond Goldin

ILLUSTRATED BY Laura Sucher

UAHC PRESS • NEW YORK, NEW YORK

With love to my brother Robert
and his family—my sister-in-law, Diana,
and my niece, Rachel
—B. D. G.

To my sons and
dearest models, T., J. and G.
—L. S.

"Can't we put a real roof on it? Just this once?" Daniel pleaded as he helped his father carry the boards to build the sukkah, the little hut his family put up each year for Sukkot.

"No," said Papa, who hammered the boards together. "There's a reason we don't have a real roof on the sukkah."

"But Grandpa has a cough and can't come. Just me and Naomi will be sleeping in it and . . ." Daniel thought about night and the sky showing through the top of the hut. Could a bear climb up there? Or a wolf? Daniel shivered.

"We have enough boards for a roof, Papa."

"That's not the point," said Papa. "A sukkah is different from a house. When we're in the sukkah, we're supposed to see the sky through the roof. And if it rains, we're supposed to feel the rain. So we can remember." Papa stood back to admire the hut with its door cut in one side and a window in another.

"Remember what?" asked Daniel. All he could remember were the scary sounds he heard in the sukkah last year. Grandpa sang him lullabies so he could fall asleep. His sister Naomi wouldn't sing him lullabies—that was for sure.

"We remember how our ancestors left Egypt in a hurry, thousands of years ago," Papa answered. "How they wandered in the desert for forty years and slept in temporary shelters like this one whenever they stopped for the night."

"Oh," said Daniel. He wondered if the ancestors were afraid, too. Of the dark. And the night. And the scary noises. And of bears and wolves.

"Later, in Israel," Papa added, "the farmers built little huts like this one to sleep in during the wheat harvest."

Daniel could tell Papa wasn't going to put a real roof on the sukkah, not even this once.

Daniel tried to forget about the holes in the roof and the bears and wolves while the family made paper chains to hang inside the sukkah and drew pictures for the walls, pictures of trees and holy places and people from the Bible.

Naomi tied apples to the roof with string so they dangled in the air. Daniel and Leah piled fat squash, yellow and orange and green squash, lumpy and crooked squash on the table and in the corners of the hut.

"It's beautiful," said Daniel when they were done.

"Even nicer than last year's," said Naomi. "And this year we get to sleep in it all alone." She looked at Daniel. "Unless, of course, you're too scared."

Daniel stiffened his shoulders. "I slept in it last year, didn't I?"

Naomi snickered. "Yes, with Grandpa singing you to sleep."

"I'm not afraid of the dark anymore," Daniel said, "not since Mama bought me a night light."

"You can't have a night light in a sukkah," Naomi said. "There's no plug. Do you think our ancestors had night lights when they lived in their sukkot?"

"Maybe," Daniel said.

"Thousands of years ago?" Naomi choked back a giggle. "You must be kidding. All they had was the desert sand and rocks and whatever they brought from Egypt. Besides, you'll be scared at the first noise. You'll think there's a bear or a wolf." She made a growly face at Daniel.

"I will not," said Daniel. "Anyway, do *you* want to sleep out here all alone?"

"I could," said Naomi. "I'm not afraid of wolves or bears."

"Time for supper," called Mama from the house. "I need your help. There's lots of food to bring outside."

Daniel and Leah,
Naomi, Mama and Papa,
and all their guests ate
in the sukkah that night.
They had to wear
sweaters and their chairs
bumped against the
walls, but the air was
crisp and cool and
smelled sweet.

The food tasted so good, and the sound of their talk and laughter bounced all around them, off the walls and up through the cornstalks into the night sky.

Daniel felt full and a little sleepy after eating so much. He leaned back in his chair, thinking of long ago, of ancestors traveling in the desert, eating and talking in their sukkot, too; of the farmers too busy to go home.

Daniel felt so good and so happy that he almost wasn't afraid anymore. The sukkah felt warm and cozy all around, and if he didn't look up, he could even forget the holes in the roof.

Closing his eyes, he smelled the sweetness in the air, of fruit and spices and candles burning. Maybe it wouldn't be so bad sleeping in the sukkah.

After dinner, Daniel helped
bring all the dishes back into the
house. Soon the sukkah was
empty again, of people and
food, sounds and light.

Naomi carried out her blankets and pillow and put them in
a corner of the sukkah. She
came looking for Daniel.

"Are you ready?" she asked.
"Yes," said Daniel, even though
deep down inside he still wasn't sure.

He carried out his blankets and pillow and his teddy bear. Then he settled down next to Naomi, twisting and turning in his blanket bed on the ground.

"I can't go to sleep with all your moving around," complained Naomi.

"All right," said Daniel. He closed his eyes and tried to lie still.

It wasn't quiet for long.

Whoo. The wind started up. It blew through the cornstalks on the roof and shook the walls. Clack clack. Creeek creeek.

"It's just the wind," whispered Naomi.

"Why are you whispering?" asked Daniel. "Are you scared, too?"

"Of course not," she said.
But her voice squeaked a little.

Oof oof. Oof oof.
Daniel sat straight up.
It was hard being an
ancestor in the hut, in
the dark. And scary.
"Is that a wolf?"
Daniel whispered. He
thought he felt Naomi
shiver next to him. He
grabbed his stuffed bear.

Naomi sat up, too.
They listened together.

"It's just a dog," she finally said. "I think." She buried her-
self in her blankets, pulling them tightly around her.

Daniel lay down next to her. But he didn't close his eyes.
"It's spooky out here," he said.
Naomi didn't answer.
Naomi was asleep. Lucky Naomi, thought Daniel.

Daniel lay awake, his eyes searching every corner of the hut. He began to see faces where the squash were supposed to be. Mean, lumpy, grinning faces. There was one over there in the corner. And one on the table by the door. And one pointing at him through the window.

Daniel stood up, clutching his bear. It was too hard being an ancestor. He thought about his room, the familiar shapes in its corners, and the night light by his bed.

Just then, Naomi put out her hand and tugged at Daniel.

"Don't go. Please," she said softly. "Keep me company."

"I'm too scared," he said. "Aren't you?"

"A little," Naomi admitted. She was quiet for a moment, staring at the sky through the sukkah roof.

"You know, Daniel, maybe I was wrong. Maybe our ancestors did have night lights in the desert."

"But you said there were no plugs . . . ."

"I know, I know. But. . ."

Naomi held up her covers. "Slide in right next to me and look up. See? They had the first kind of night lights."

Daniel lay down next to his sister and looked up. Through the branches and the stalks, he saw stars, tiny, bright night light stars, and one gigantic night light moon. They were the same moon and stars the wanderers in the desert and the farmers in the fields had seen at night through their sukkah roofs.

"See what I mean?" asked Naomi.

"Uh-huh," answered Daniel. He felt warm and cozy now, next to Naomi.

So, instead of looking at the shadows or listening to the dogs and the wind, Daniel and Naomi watched the lights above them, thinking of ancestors and of candles glowing on sukkah tabletops. And soon they fell asleep.

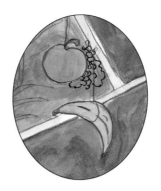

Author's Note

Sukkot, also called the Feast of Tabernacles of the Festival of Booths, is a weeklong fall holiday beginning on the fifteenth day of the Hebrew month of Tishrei (September or October). To celebrate Sukkot, Jews all over the world build little huts, or sukkot, with leafy branches for roofs. (Sukkot in Hebrew is plural. Sukkah is singular).

In the days of the ancient Temple in Jerusalem, the Israelites celebrated three pilgrimage festivals. Passover, the first pilgrimage festival in the historical cycle, commemorated the Exodus of the Israelites from Egypt and from slavery. Shavuot, the second pilgrimage festival, celebrated God giving the law to Moses at Mount Sinai. Sukkot completed the cycle by marking the forty years that the Israelites wandered in the desert after receiving the law, before they entered the Promised Land. To celebrate Sukkot, the Israelites traveled to the Holy City from all over the country, bringing the fruits of their labors to offer to God.

Though Jews can no longer make offerings in the ancient Temple on Sukkot, they build little huts to eat in and sometimes to sleep in during the festival. In this way, they commemorate the forty years of wandering. Building a hut also helps Jews remember how the ancient desert wanderers settled in the Promised Land and became farmers. These farmers built huts near their crops at harvesttime so they could pick the crops quickly and watch over them in case of bad weather or theft.

A sukkah provides temporary shelter and therefore lets in much more rain and sun, wind and storm than does a more permanent structure like a house. Being in a sukkah reminds us of how vulnerable we are to the forces of nature, and how our lives are dependent on and enriched by the natural world.

—BARBARA DIAMOND GOLDIN